# The Elephant in the Room

*It was six men of Indostan,*
*To learning much inclined,*
*Who went to see the Elephant,*
*(Though all of them were blind),*
*That each by observation*
*Might satisfy his mind.*

—JOHN GODFREY

http://www.TheElephantintheRoom.net

ISBN: 978-0-9793654-0-9

Cover and Interior Design: Desktop Miracles, Inc.

This novel is a work of fiction. Any references to real people, events, establishments, organizations, or locales are intended only to give the fiction a sense of reality and authenticity. Other names, characters, places, and incidents portrayed herein are either the product of the author's imagination or are used fictitiously.

Publisher's Cataloging-In-Publication Data
(Prepared by The Donohue Group, Inc.)

Baker, Ed., pseud.
    The elephant in the room : sharing the secrets for pursuing real financial success / Ed Baker.
        p. ; cm.
    ISBN: 978-0-9793654-0-9
    1. Finance, Personal—Fiction. 2. Wealth—Fiction. I. Title.
PS3602.A5862 E54    2007

                                                                813.6

Printed in the United States of America

# *The* Elephant
## *in the*
# Room

SHARING THE SECRETS
FOR PURSUING
REAL FINANCIAL SUCCESS

**Ed Baker**

# Contents

*Preface*
9

*Introduction*
15

ONE
The First Meeting
19

TWO
Attitude
37

THREE
Knowledge
55

FOUR
Financial Beliefs
65

FIVE

Values
83

SIX

Goals
95

SEVEN

Patience & Discipline
107

EIGHT

The Plan
117

NINE

A Financial Planning Model
129

*Epilogue*
137

# Preface

I SAT DOWN ON THE five o'clock business shuttle to Boston and buckled my seat belt.

The flight was fully loaded, and passengers shuttled past until nearly one hundred fifty seats were completely filled. Most were business travelers it seemed, on their way to one meeting or another. The rest was a mix of travelers.

We lingered at the gate, and I checked my watch as the departure time passed. I had traveled all over the world, and this wasn't characteristic of a normal flight. Normally, the airlines were concerned about pushing back as soon as possible to meet their on-time departure goals.

After about fifteen minutes, a voice squeaked over the intercom.

"Ladies and gentlemen, I'd like to apologize, but our pilots haven't shown up yet. They were on an earlier connection that's been delayed."

It seemed that the passengers were ready, but the pilots hadn't shown up yet. We were all ready and willing to head to our destination, but there was no one to get us there.

What if your financial life is the same way? You might be ready and willing to begin building wealth and a solid financial future, but you may not have any way to get there. You may know what to do, or have some sense of what to do, but without a coach, you may never get there. Most Americans struggle with the idea of planning for their financial future. A *Wall Street Journal* article reported that 70 percent of Americans live paycheck to paycheck! Their major concern is survival, and it's hard to grasp the possibility of saving money. As we go to press with this story, the U.S. government just announced that our personal savings rate for the last year was minus 1 percent, the lowest in 74 years. As a people, we spend all our income plus 1 percent more, either drawing on savings or piling on more debt. It's bad.

The lethal combination of a lack of financial know-how combined with an inability to discern or accept the difference between material "wants" versus "needs" creates a situation where many American families find themselves unable to see an achievable path to long-term financial success. Many American households are in debt simply because family members have seen something that someone else has and they want it too ... right here, right now! That behavior pattern repeats itself over and over again until, before long, the credit-card balance has increased to an unmanageable amount.

Why is it that so many Americans are in trouble? Money ranks right up there as one of the most important, if not the most important, personal drives in most people's lives. It's the number-one underlying cause of divorce in America today and a threat to emotional harmony. There's an old saying that money can't buy happiness, but when you have enough of it, you're free to focus on all of the other aspects of your life that bring you joy. When you don't have enough money to pay the bills and you're stressing over how to make ends meet, chances are you aren't happy, your spouse isn't happy, and if you have children, they will feel the tension, too.

Building wealth means focusing on more than just making money. It's about working for the things that make life gratifying and creating a healthy and well-balanced lifestyle for you and your family. Wealth building means developing a financial legacy that will ensure that your future is secure. Peace and confidence follow.

One thing I've learned during my time in the financial services industry is that the single greatest determiner of an individual's success is his or her own *behavior*. This fact is good news, because behavior is one variable we can all control and change. There are specific traits and behaviors we see in people who are successful with money, and there are also specific, identifiable behavior patterns of those who persistently struggle.

If you're really serious about your financial legacy and saving for all of the things that are important to you and your family's future, consider the role a financial planner can play in your life. Even the best athletes and highest achievers in the world have coaches to teach them the principles of success. You may already be pretty good with money, but there are probably some things you aren't aware of. A financial planner may open your eyes. It happens often. Financial advisors have to study what's going on in the industry every day—do you really have time for that? Tiger Woods is one of the best golfers in the world, and even he has a coach! Many of the top CEOs in the world have coaches who help them grow in selected areas. Having a professional on your team to guide the process is one of the best decisions you can make.

Where are you in the quest to build a secure financial future? Most families today save less, invest less, and borrow more, creating stress on their relationships and within the families. But the good news is that your family doesn't have to be one of them! You can start today and lead your family to a legacy of strength and a mind-set of building wealth.

It is my hope that you find this book to be a valuable resource that will help you clarify and achieve your goals and dreams.

LAMAR SMITH
Chairman Emeritus
First Command Financial Services Inc.

# Introduction

My name is Michael Davidson. I never imagined I'd find myself looking for advice at a time in my life when it seemed I had already achieved so much. Sure, I had needed advice during my younger years and in college, but now I was facing down thirty, with a wife and two kids. Madison was five, and our baby, Alexandra, was about to turn two. Time was flying by, and life was good. Jennifer, my wife, had been so supportive of my new career. From the beginning of our marriage, it seemed she had always been in my corner, cheering me on through every job interview, promotion, and new project. Despite the late nights and travel my job required, she was always there, taking care of the kids, juggling schedules, and managing our life. So what was the problem?

The problem is hard to pinpoint. The arguments started small, a purchase here, an expenditure there. She'd buy something, I'd question it, and she would get defensive. I'd buy a new suit for work, and it seemed as if she'd resent it. She wanted things for the house; I needed things for my job. A new briefcase, a tie. There never seemed to be enough money at the end of the month, despite my long hours. I suppose if there were, we never would have argued at all. At times, Jennifer resented working, but at other times, she seemed to love her teaching job. I just wished we had more options and more money.

It was after one tense discussion that I decided I had nowhere else to turn. I had to start making some changes, fast, before Jennifer and I grew apart. I had to take care of my family, develop a plan. I was bound and determined to make it all work, and I decided to call Aunt Katherine.

Aunt Kath was in her seventies, and she was about the only person I knew who was completely content and comfortable. By comfortable, I mean that she didn't have to worry about money. It seemed as if she had planned well. Most of the retirees or widows I knew of were just barely getting by, but Aunt Katherine was taking amazing trips to South America, to Europe, and to Hawaii with a seniors group she was involved in. Aunt Katherine had it together, and as hard as it was to admit it, I wanted to have it together too, but I didn't. I figured that if anyone could help me, she could.

ONE

# The First Meeting

THE AFTERNOON AUNT KATHERINE and I scheduled for our first lunch meeting turned out to be a chamber-of-commerce day. I slid the Ford Explorer out of the garage into the brilliant sunshine and drove down the winding roads leading out of our neighborhood. I considered how the next hour would play out and what I would say. I had been anxious all week and even started making a list of the questions I'd ask. I knew she'd be straight with me and give me the answers I needed. She and Uncle George had done pretty well, and lately it seemed more and more obvious to me that I had a lot to learn.

When Uncle George retired from the U.S. Air Force, he and Aunt Katherine settled down in a nice, upscale neighborhood in Denver. They had a beautiful home and a great life. I had heard that George had made some investments that paid off well, but they never talked much about it. After Uncle George died, Aunt Katherine stayed in their comfortable home. Now, five years later, she was busy with new hobbies, like a travel club she had joined. It had taken me several weeks to schedule a lunch with her because she had been out of the country, on a trip with a group of women her age.

I arrived at the restaurant at 12:20, ten minutes earlier than planned. I scanned the room for a quiet table and found one back in the corner, facing a window. From there you could see the hustle and bustle of pedestrians on Main, some who worked in the surrounding stores and markets. Downtown Denver had grown, and my corporate office had decided to relocate there, lucky for me. My new job, selling pharmaceuticals, had put me into a pay category I'd never been in. Even so, with two kids under five, it sure didn't seem like Jennifer and I were getting anywhere. After six years of marriage, we had our first home but had barely saved anything at all. I looked out the window and saw Aunt Katherine walking briskly up the sidewalk. She was tanned and smiling. She turned into the restaurant and found me right away.

"Michael! How great to see you!" We embraced and she kissed my cheek.

"It's good to see you too," I said.

We sat down and waited for the waitress. Aunt Katherine took a sip from her water glass and leaned back in her chair.

"How are the children?"

"Wonderful," I replied.

"And Jennifer?"

"Great. She's teaching first grade and loves it."

"Good," she said. "You know Michael, I've been concerned since I got your message. Are you and Jennifer having financial troubles?"

"I hope I didn't alarm you. It's nothing serious," I said. "But I've been wanting to call you about this for the longest time. Thanks for agreeing to meet so soon after you got back to town."

"No problem at all. My cruise was fantastic. We traveled all around the islands down in the Caribbean. It was wonderful. But enough about the trip. What's going on with you?"

I leaned forward. "I can't help but look at someone like you and think I'm failing, Aunt Kath. Jen and I are just squeaking by." I cleared my throat. "You're so lucky to be financially set ... to have money. You travel any time you want, buy anything you want ... You have a great life."

The waitress interrupted and took our order. I ordered a cheeseburger, and Aunt Katherine ordered the Wednesday special, soup and salad.

Aunt Katherine slipped her napkin to her lap and looked me straight in the eye. "Haven't you heard that money can't buy happiness?"

"Yes, I've heard that, but quite honestly, I think it could buy me some happiness. Happiness and freedom."

"Michael, you and I aren't in agreement here. I believe that money is just a tool," she said. "It's not what life is all about. Money in itself can't make you happy."

"I know, Aunt Kath. But I can't help but feel as if I'd be a whole lot happier with some extra breathing room each month." My shoulders felt heavy. "We're not unhappy, but we're stressed."

Aunt Katherine looked me straight in the eye. "You have a beautiful family, a wonderful wife, so much to look forward to. You're too young to be stressed about money or any other reason. Now is the time for you to earn and save and build for your future. Knowing what you want your life to stand for and seeing how your financial success can fuel that is powerful, Michael. But money in itself is not powerful enough to bring true joy."

I leaned forward. "Honestly, I'll just get right to the point. I need some answers, Aunt Kath. Real answers. It's about our finances. Jennifer and I always seem to end the month with less money than we need to pay the bills. We're doing really well for people our age, so it just doesn't seem right. When I think about the things we've got ahead, like the expense of the children's college, it makes me wonder how we're going to do it." I let out a deep breath. It felt good. I hadn't talked to anyone else about our money situation.

Aunt Katherine leaned back. "Well, you've come to the right place," she said warmly.

"I thought so. Those lessons George would try to instill in me about preparing for the future didn't go completely over my head. I know it's important," I said. "I just don't know how to do it."

She smiled. "George really was all about being prepared. He didn't just talk about it, he prepared well, and he made sure that I was taken care of after he was gone."

"I want to be that kind of man," I said, and I did. I wanted to be there for my family. I didn't want my kids to have to worry about how they would pay for college when the time was right, like I had to. I wanted everything to be set and secure. But right now our situation seemed to be far from that.

"Your Uncle George worked hard to build his legacy, Michael. That was important to him. Managing his finances well was only a small part of that."

I shook my head. "I want to build a legacy," I said. "I want the kids to be secure, and we're doing well enough, but right now it seems like we're living month to month."

"Well, you've got a great job," she said. "But that's not enough."

"I'm beginning to think you're right."

Aunt Katherine then said, "Michael I have loved you all your life and now I can add great respect to that." I sat looking at her and she went on. "Too many people lack the courage to overcome the temptation to deny their shortfalls and avoid confronting their future realistically. It can be scary, but you are a man of courage and I respect that greatly."

Aunt Katherine fumbled around in her purse. "I want you to read something," she said. "It's something that George had on his dresser. He kept it right under his money clip. It was one of his favorite things, I guess, and I grabbed it after you and I spoke the other day and you said you were having some problems. I thought you might want to read it." She opened a piece of crumpled paper and pushed it across the table.

"What's this?"

"Have you ever heard the poem about the blind men and the elephant?"

"No."

"It's a story about something huge that no one is getting right. The six blind men come up to an elephant, and each one interprets it differently. One feels the elephant's side and thinks it's a wall. The second feels its tusk and thinks they've come upon a spear. All six of the men envision the elephant differently."

I looked down. The words were typewritten in black ink. "What does this *poem* have to do with anything?"

"It's not about the poem, Michael. As it relates to your situation, I see the elephant as a metaphor for behavior. There's an elephant in the room, and no one understands it. *Behavior* is the elephant in the room when it comes to financial success. It is not what you know or intend. It's what you *do* that determines the outcome."

"I don't follow you."

"I know," she said. "But you will." She smiled. "The funny thing is, Michael, that lots of people don't know how to figure a way out, because they don't clearly understand the situation. You've got financial issues, but do you really understand what's behind them?"

I stared at her blankly. "I don't know."

"Well, what do you think are important issues in establishing a sound financial situation?" she asked. "Have you given it some thought?"

"Of course I have." I sat for a while and thought about it more. "Making a lot of money, for one. Investing in the right things, for two. I see those as two keys to financial success."

"Maybe," she said.

*The most important factor that will contribute to long-term financial success for your family isn't making a lot of money.
The most important factor is* **behavior.**

"What do you mean maybe? You're telling me it's not important to make money?"

"Well, you need money to live, no doubt. But the most important factor that will contribute to long-term financial success for your family isn't making a lot of money. A lot of people make a lot of money, Michael, and still have significant financial issues. The most important factor is *behavior*."

"Behavior! What are you talking about?"

"Think about it," Aunt Katherine said. "It doesn't really matter how much money you bring in if you don't keep it. If you're careless or reckless, you may not hold on to the money you earn. We need to spend time thinking and talking about the elements that guide your behavior."

I nodded. This WAS something I had to think about. Jennifer and I had just had our first major argument about money. Our approaches to financial issues were certainly different.

"Don't underestimate how the values that drive your behavior will determine your future," Aunt Katherine said.

I sat silent for a minute and wondered what she meant. I thought about the things that could be destructive, where money was concerned. Luckily Jennifer and I both had great jobs, and we were building a family together. We knew what we wanted and had pretty good habits, but we were far from prepared for the future. I had heard about the bad things that happened to other people. Loss of employment, a sudden disability like a back problem that left the older regional manager unable to walk for long periods of time. Last I heard, he was still out of work and collecting disability, but he worried about what would happen when his disability checks stopped coming.

"Behavior is something that can be modified," Aunt Katherine said. "That's the good news. If there's *too much month and not enough money*, chances are you may need to make some changes. It might not even be the big things you're spending on. It may not be that you play golf and that Jennifer likes nice things or that the kids need nice new clothes. It may just be that you need to plan better to come out ahead.

"Do you and Jennifer talk about your financial goals? Do you know what you want?"

I thought for a moment. "Sure, we talk . . . but not really in detail about the money. That's my area to take care of. She takes care of the kids and everything else around the house."

"But she earns money too," Aunt Katherine said.

"Well . . . yes she does. We both wish she could stay home full-time, but her job as a teacher really helps our family make ends meet. And she loves it. She's really good with kids."

Aunt Katherine took a bite of her salad. "You have to talk about finances," she said. "It's important."

"I don't know where to start, I guess."

"George always said that you need to start with your values and your vision. Start making a list together of all the things you want to accomplish in your life. Next, make a list of how you will pay for it. Sitting down with Jennifer would be a good first step. You will learn some things about each other that you did not know. Michael, don't be surprised if this project turns out to be a lot more difficult than you might think. It sounds simple; but for us, it took an advisor to help determine what we truly valued about our lives and how our values would shape our financial journey."

"And after we develop the list?"

"I've got an idea," she said. "How about we meet every week for the next several weeks, and I'll share everything I know about preparing for a sound financial future. I'm an old bird, Michael," she winked. "You might learn something."

I thought about the vacations she'd taken, the comfortable home, the nice car, and clothes. She had the freedom to travel and see relatives, and it seemed as if she had everything she needed. She and Uncle George had done well.

"That sounds great," I said.

"I'll give you an assignment to work on each week, and you can go home and talk it over with Jennifer. I'm happy to help out however I can," she said. She looked into my eyes. "Listen to me. What most people don't understand, and what usually turns out to be the elephant in the room, is their *behavior*. It affects everything in your life, including the way you earn, spend, and save. So in each of the next several weeks, we're going to reflect on a specific element of behavior as it relates to financial success and better understand how that element impacts your behavior and its relationship to your financial future."

I leaned back and crossed my arms. "What's the topic next week, coach?"

Aunt Katherine smiled. "Next week we'll start with *attitude*."

"Attitude?"

"Yes, attitude."

"I think I have a pretty good attitude." I said.

"We'll see about that," Aunt Katherine said, grinning. "Next week we'll talk about the attitude you have toward money and the attitude you have toward your financial future. So here's your homework: think about your attitude toward money and finances and write down your thoughts."

"Okay," I said.

"But don't do it alone, Michael. I'm starting to feel as if I'm only getting one side of the story."

"What do you mean?"

"Well, you're here and Jennifer's not. You have one attitude about money, but Jennifer probably has her own feelings about things. George and I both were involved in our financial affairs. We did it together. You can't properly or adequately prepare for your family's future if only one of you is doing it. Do you and Jennifer have the same attitudes about money?"

I stared at her blankly.

"Think about it," she said. "We'll talk about it next week."

"Same time, same place?" I asked.

She smiled. "Wouldn't miss it for the world."

Aunt Katherine stood and waved the waitress over. Before I could protest, she paid for our lunch and hugged me good-bye. She blew me a kiss through the window and pressed the remote for her car, causing the lights on the front to flash. I watched her and smiled as she slid the little sports car away from the curb.

*Now that is how life should be*, I thought. Navigating through life's peaks and valleys with a good plan and a solid future.

## Behavior

Behavior is the "elephant in the room" when it comes to financial success.

Courage is needed to view the past and future realistically.

Think about my behaviors and how they might affect our financial situation. Talk it over with Jen. What are our attitudes toward money? Are they different?

Building a sound financial future entails more than just making money or investing it wisely.

There are specific traits, or behaviors, that people who are successful in their finances adopt and incorporate into their lives. What traits and attitudes affect the way we earn, spend, and save?

# TWO

# Attitude

I BROUGHT JENNIFER WITH ME to the restaurant on the second Wednesday and led her to the same booth Aunt Katherine and I had shared the week before. A few minutes later, Aunt Katherine showed up, grinning with surprise.

"Jennifer!" She held my wife's hands and kissed her cheek. They slid into the booth, and I pondered the variety on the menu.

The waitress stopped by. "Ready to order?" she asked.

Aunt Katherine ordered the Wednesday special as she and Jennifer sat together, looking through some new photos of the kids.

I considered the selections. "There are just so many," I said. "Any recommendations on what's best?"

The waitress just stared at me, pen poised over the small pad in her hand. I looked down at the menu again.

"I like the broiled haddock," the girl said. "If you like fish."

"That's expensive," Jennifer said. We exchanged glances. "I'll have the Caesar salad," my wife added.

I closed the menu. "Give me a grilled cheese."

Aunt Katherine smiled. "Did you have a good week?"

"Yes. Thanks. It was extremely busy at work, but when I had time, I thought a lot about our conversation."

"Did you have time to do your homework?"

I shook my head. "Nope, sorry. I didn't. It was just too crazy at work, and Jennifer seemed to be busy with the baby every time I thought about talking to her about attitude."

I held up my notebook. The lined page was white and blank. At the very top I had written one word. *Attitude.* "That's as far as I got."

Aunt Katherine just smiled. "That's okay," she said. "But this is important, Michael. I'm making a commitment to you for these meetings and need you to be committed, too."

"I just couldn't think of anything. Nothing came to mind. I guess I didn't know what you were looking for."

"I wasn't *looking* for anything, Michael. It's not a test."

"Then what's the point?"

She sighed. "Unless you believe you can change your life—you won't. That's the point. I can't force you to want to think about your attitude and your habits." She took another sip of her iced tea. Outside the window the sidewalk was crowded. Businesspeople spilled in and out of shops for the lunch hour. She turned to me. Jennifer sat silently and listened.

"Michael, maybe we're not approaching this the right way. Let's start from the beginning. What comes to mind when you think of the word *attitude?*"

I sat silent for a while. "Well," I said finally, "I guess you either have a good one or a bad one. That's about all I can think of."

"That's certainly true. You can make a choice to have a good attitude or a bad one, but there's a lot more to it. Attitude is your general thought or mind-set about certain things in your life. Your attitude is the foundation for a lot of different behaviors and actions."

"Okay . . . and?"

"And it's important to understand your attitude about money and your financial future, including the underlying feelings you have about earning, spending, and saving. If you don't have the right attitude, you won't be successful. But if you have the right attitude, Michael, and if Jennifer does too, your chances for a successful financial future are greatly enhanced."

"So what's the right attitude?"

"There's no easy answer to that one. First, understanding the principles of financial security is all about maturity. Being mature about money means having the ability to see

*Your attitude is the foundation for a
lot of different behaviors and actions.
With the right attitude your
chances for financial success
are greatly enhanced.*

the long-term implications of current choices. Kind of like having a big-picture view of your life versus a snapshot of only one day or month of your life. Make sense?"

"Sure . . ."

"Makes sense to me!" Jennifer said.

"You've probably known people who have to buy everything they see. People who see a friend get a new car and then have to have a new car themselves may lack maturity, and often are short-term thinkers. One element of immaturity in financial matters is the inability to delay short-term gratification for long-term benefit."

"Like patience?"

Jennifer sat forward. "Aunt Katherine, I think you're more patient than we are," she said. "About most things."

Aunt Katherine smiled. "Maturity and patience go hand in hand. They are qualities of someone who wants to build wealth. So is an attitude of learning."

"Why learning?" I asked. "Isn't there a point where we should just dive in and take control of our lives?"

"You have to be open and willing to learn in order to gain knowledge. Experience is a great teacher, but only if you are paying attention. A lot of people think they know everything about financial matters, so they aren't willing to learn anything new."

"Do you think we're open to learning?"

"Yes, I do. You're here, aren't you?"

I smiled and thought about the round chip Uncle George had often played with between his fingers and used for his magic tricks when we were young. It looked like a coin, only it was wooden and had something written across the front of it. He kept it in his pocket for those family gatherings when the kids were gathered in the living room around his chair, watching the magic coin appear from behind someone's ear. One day he let me hold it. The lettering on the front said "TO IT," and he explained to me how most people procrastinate, and that this wooden coin was his reminder not to—his reminder to "get around to it." I didn't understand the joke at the time.

"The wrong attitudes can prevent you from gaining the knowledge that can change your financial future," Aunt Katherine continued. "Like impatience or procrastination or irresponsibility. As I said last week, it's likely that you have one attitude about financial issues, but Jennifer probably has her own feelings about things. You need to talk about these things, because you can't properly or adequately prepare for your family's future if you don't do it together."

Jennifer and I looked at each other.

"But the first place to start is with yourself," Aunt Katherine said.

"How so?"

"One way to start would be to look at the things you've purchased in the last three months or so. That tells a big story about your attitude about finances. You'd be surprised."

I nodded and thought about the tie I'd purchased with the Visa card and the way I had paid for the electric bill on credit because we didn't have the money in our bank account at the time. Now I was getting curious about the whole thing. Maybe I should have done my homework.

"If you both think about the things you purchased in the last three months, you'll be able to see how often an attitude of 'needing' something really just boils down to an attitude of 'wanting' something."

I looked out the window. It seemed like there was always something we wanted. Something we had found a way to justify needing.

I glanced at Jennifer. "I'm not looking forward to those discussions."

"Me neither," she said. "We fight about the electric bill. How are we going to talk calmly about all of the plans for our money?"

"It will be difficult. But you're both adults, and you'll both have to have the courage to identify what you need to change and then do what is needed. Once you identify the roadblocks and attitudes that are causing you to get in a bind, you can change your choices for the better as you learn more and gain experience. You can't follow the crowd, guys. The herd mentality won't give you financial security."

She paused as her words sank in.

"Doing what everyone else is doing will provide some comfort, but eventually you will end up ... well, in the pack ... which in America means in the 90 percent who do not achieve long-term financial success!"

"I'm tired of keeping up with the Joneses," Jennifer said. "We aren't the Joneses."

"Keeping up with the neighbors is a flawed attitude," she said. "We live in this culture of instant gratification, and it seems like everyone has a cell phone, a nice new grill, a new car. Remember the saying, 'He who dies with the most toys wins'?"

I laughed.

"That gets a lot of people in trouble, Michael. That's a flawed attitude. It leads to financial distress, not financial success."

"It seems here lately we've just been surviving, living month to month despite some good raises the last few years. There hasn't been a lot of extra spending. We haven't been getting crazy. And Jennifer's pretty good about clipping coupons for groceries."

"That's good, but there's a lot more to it. Some couples stay in a survival mode and never make it out. They have a lot of debt, and it keeps accumulating. In that kind of scenario, it's hard to address long-range financial success. It seems hard to plan. But in that case, planning is important."

"We don't have extra money or energy right now ..."

"There's no way to get on solid ground and start building wealth unless you start addressing long-term financial issues now. No pain, no gain ... an attitude pertinent to financial success by the way." She smiled and took a sip of her water. I took notes on my pad, writing down the words *No pain, no gain.*

Aunt Kath saw my note and said, "Let me encourage you ... done right, small pain can yield great gain."

"Well," she said setting down her water glass, "I guess we're done for the day."

I checked my watch. "Time flies with you, Aunt Kath."

"Time flies, Michael. You have to reevaluate your attitude and start thinking about your future. You have to plan now."

"I know . . . we've talked about saving and investments and stocks—"

"Those are the easy things to focus on, but you also have to think about securing your kids' future. Things like insurance." She looked away, into the crowded restaurant. "You know, Michael, George was a smart man. We planned for our financial future and stuck to the plan, and we had help along the way. We were able to learn about some of the factors of financial success."

"Like having a good attitude?" Jennifer joked.

"Yes. But attitude is just one element that factors into the concept of behavior. It's behavior that drives success."

I sat and listened. It dawned on me then that she was making a lot of sense.

"There are several more pieces of the puzzle that you probably don't see clearly right now," Aunt Katherine said. "But that's okay. At least you're ready to start. How about you, Jennifer?"

"I'm ready to start as soon as we get home," said Jen.

"Good," she said. "This is important, and you both need to start thinking about a plan. You know, George and I weren't always so smart about financial issues."

"You weren't?"

She shook her head. "No, unfortunately we weren't. You know that your uncle was an air force pilot, and well, most pilots, by their very nature, tend to live for the moment." She smiled. "I loved that quality about him, but that's how we lived early in our marriage. We spent everything we made, in constant search of a fun time, traveling . . ." Her voice trailed off.

I looked at her intently.

"One year, George's squadron suffered two crashes where the pilots were killed. We saw how unprepared the families of those pilots were—little or no savings, no insurance other than that provided by the government. The wives and children were left to struggle financially."

I sat forward in the booth, anxiously awaiting the rest of the story. My heart felt heavy.

"That was an eye-opening experience for both of us, but especially for George. He saw how our attitude of 'live for today' was detrimental. It wasn't preparing us for a sound financial future and would not provide well for me if anything happened to him or vice versa. Those accidents were a wake-up call in our life."

"What did you do?"

"We changed. We both became very serious about planning and working for a sound financial future."

I shook my head. "I had no idea."

"But nothing bad has to happen in your life for you to change. You've got an advantage, and you can start now."

"Okay! So what's next week, coach?"

Aunt Katherine smiled and stood. She waved the waitress over and handed her a twenty-dollar bill.

"Are you going to do your homework this week?" she asked.

"Yes," I groaned. "I feel like I'm back in college again. What's this week's assignment?"

"Your assignment for next week is knowledge. So think about your attitude and then pull out a blank sheet of paper and write the word *knowledge* at the top of it. Make a list of all the things you think you know about money and all the things you want to learn about."

"I got an A in economics, you know," I said. "This could be fun."

"Good," Aunt Katherine said. "It is fun. And the rewards will be great!"

## Attitude

Need to consider and constantly reconsider our attitudes regarding our financial situation.

"Wants" are <u>not</u> "needs" . . . do we recognize the difference when making financial decisions? Are we honest in our assessments?

It is time to get "a round TO IT"— in other words get started NOW on our financial future. No pain, no gain.

Procrastination is a killer when it comes to pursuing long-term financial success.

## Procrastination

If we started investing $300/month now for the next 30 years and it earned a net interest of 8%, at the end of 30 years we'd have $425,400. BUT, if we delayed just two years and therefore only saved for 28 years, we'd have $357,900—Investing $7200 less (24 months at $300/month) creates a $67,500 difference! That certainly shows the power of time when considering compound interest.

TO IT

# THREE

# Knowledge

T HE WEEK BETWEEN MY next meeting with Aunt Katherine was enlightening. Somehow it seemed I thought about financial issues every day. Money going in, money going out. I snapped at Jennifer once at the drive-through when she bought an extra cheeseburger for the kid who mowed our yard. He had been out mowing all day without a lunch break, and she felt sorry for him. But I didn't think it was time to start being charitable when we didn't have any money left over at the end of the month.

I drove to work and thought about money. I drove home and thought about money, always calculating. I lay in bed that week and calculated how much I'd earn that month and how much we needed for bills.

Why isn't there a money bible that everyone can read and follow? I wondered about this and why things had to seem so complex. Why couldn't there just be a manual somewhere that gave you all the answers?

Jennifer and I met Aunt Katherine on Wednesday with a renewed purpose. Her words had stayed with me all week, and this time, I had done my homework. *People's behavior is the single greatest factor that impacts financial success*, she had said. *Think about your attitude. Think about the things you know about money and the things you don't.*

My knowledge list was long. I had a host of things I had learned about money from all those years studying up on it. I knew the stock market pretty well. I was looking forward to our lunch.

After we sat down and ordered, I pushed my homework assignment across the table. Aunt Katherine grinned. Jennifer had her list too.

"Good job!" Aunt Katherine said, smiling. She looked down at the two lists. "This is a long list," she said to me. "Seems like you two know a lot about money."

"Not as much as I thought," I admitted. "I follow stocks once in a while, and I know the value of compound interest. Things like that. But I have to admit, I don't know a thing about insurance or how to save for college."

"It's hard to know everything about it if it's not your career," Jennifer said.

"That's right," said Aunt Katherine.

I shook my head. "I know. I'm a sales guy, not a financial advisor."

"One thing a lot of people don't think about," Aunt Katherine said, "is the magnitude of their future financial needs. You know, the whole shooting match. The big picture. There are things you can't possibly grasp now that you'll need money for later."

"College, for one," said Jennifer.

"And healthcare and life insurance. And don't forget how inflation is going to affect future costs," Aunt Katherine said.

I stared at her. "You mean, this cheeseburger will cost us ten dollars in ten years?"

"Maybe. Who thought a gallon of gas would triple

in price just because of something going on overseas? Inflation is almost guaranteed, like death and taxes."

She looked serious for a moment. "My generation probably didn't do as good a job as we should have in teaching your generation the basics of financial literacy."

"So it's your fault we're having such a hard time?" I smiled.

"Well, it's a good lesson. You both have to work hard to teach your kids about financial issues. They won't learn it on their own. But you have to have the right knowledge first. You have to educate yourself and be open to learning more so you can plan accordingly."

"I feel like we're spending more than we're earning," I said. "That's the first problem."

Jennifer nodded. "I agree."

"You're not alone," she said. "Just the other day I read that the whole country is spending more than they're saving. Did you know that in 2006 the national savings rate was a *negative* 1 percent?"

"How is that possible?"

"Well kids, there are probably a lot of scientific explanations, but I think it generally boils down to the fact that we're all spending more than we make, which means we're probably spending savings or running up more debt. Behaviors are linked to outcomes, after all. If your behavior or work ethic is poor, your savings ethic will be too, meaning, how you think and act will affect how much you can earn and save."

I wrote furiously, filling up the page. I tried to capture everything she said. Something about the link between behavior and wealth was intriguing. After all, behaviors could be modified. All we had to do was make a choice, a commitment to change, and adopt good, healthy behaviors that would affect our financial future.

"And the amount of debt carried by families is rising."

"How do you know all of this? You must watch the money channel," asked Jennifer.

"Oh, I couldn't do it on my own. I still meet with our financial advisor frequently."

"You're smart. Why do you meet with her so often?"

"I've found that wisdom often is as much about what you don't know as what you do know. When I was your age, I might have thought I knew it all. But I've found that an attitude of learning is important for your entire life. Everyone needs help—no one knows everything about everything."

"How do you know who to go to?" I asked.

"Good question. A good idea would be to pick your knowledge sources carefully and verify independently the points that seem important. It's the same concept as a team. Think of it as your financial intelligence network. Eventually your knowledge will become part of your core habits and lifestyle. But you both have to have similar attitudes about how to approach your financial future in order to make it work."

"Sounds smart."

"My financial advisor also keeps me current on what's going on with my finances as well as any changes in laws or other things that might affect my financial well-being. I can't afford to mess around at my age."

"You're only as old as you feel, right?" Jennifer said.

"Well, actually no. That's a myth, and it brings up a good point. Next week, we should talk about beliefs and myths and the things that people believe that aren't true. You're only as old as you feel is just one of those catchy sayings that people like to throw around, Jennifer. I don't want to sound maudlin, sweetie, but you're as old as you are. You can't turn back the clock. You need to prepare now, because you've only got so many years left here on earth."

"Gee, that sounds uplifting." I smiled, and when I looked up, she had her head back, laughing, and one hand over her mouth. She stopped and pointed a perfectly man-icured nail at me.

"There's much more to financial success than knowl-edge," Aunt Katherine said. "But knowledge, or a lack of it, will influence how you behave financially. All of these elements we're talking about will make sense in the end."

"I hope so. For our family," I said somberly.

"Yes," Aunt Katherine said. "For your family and your own peace of mind and self-satisfaction."

"So what's our homework?" I asked, pen poised and ready to write.

"Beliefs," she said. "Next week we are going to focus on financial beliefs."

I wrote the words down across the top of the page. FINANCIAL BELIEFS.

"We'll talk about the truths, beliefs, and misconceptions people have about financial issues. Things that can lead them to a high amount of debt and a lifestyle that prevents wealth from accumulating."

I nodded. It sounded good to me. "So, you want us to sit down and make a list of all the 'beliefs,' we have about money?"

"Now you're starting to get it!"

"But how does that differ from knowledge?" Jennifer asked.

"Knowledge is about what you've learned and is based on fact. Financial beliefs, on the other hand, are more opinion than fact. They can develop over time with little or no factual evidence and can have a significant impact on your financial situation."

"Hmm. Still not grasping it. Help me out," I said.

"Well, with knowledge, and the list I asked you to

make—the first thing on your list was that stocks are important. Stocks can be a good investment, of course, but not always. So your knowledge about money may not be totally accurate or compete."

"And beliefs?"

"The beliefs assignment is different. Your list should focus on what you and Jennifer believe is true about money. The things you hear that you believe to be true, not necessarily things you've learned, but things you believe."

"Well, I have one good example. My boss at work always says that you have to have several credit cards to build good credit."

Aunt Katherine smiled. "Good example. Because that's a false belief that a lot of us have. Credit cards are just debt, after all. We won't get into that this week, but you're off to a good start. That's a perfect example of a belief."

She waved the waitress over for the check. "These are just some of the elements of behavior," she said. "By the time we're done, you'll be a financial warrior! You'll be ready to lay out a plan for your entire future."

## Knowledge

We need to have a sound foundation of knowledge about financial issues.

Pick my knowledge sources wisely

You cannot "know it all," especially if you're not a financial professional. Aunt Kath is pretty sharp with regard to financial issues, yet she uses a financial advisor.

Wisdom sometimes is as much about what you don't know as it is about what you do know.

# FOUR

# Financial Beliefs

On Saturday, the dishwasher broke, and I spent an hour inside it trying to fix the plumbing, with Jennifer and the kids standing around me, watching. Truth is, I never was much of a handyman, and I grew frustrated until finally I had to give in and call the plumber, who charged us time and a half for a Saturday visit. By Monday, I had found myself thinking a lot about the discussion with Aunt Katherine, and I had to confess that her wisdom was refreshing. I couldn't ask the guys at work about money, after all. I was a top earner on our sales team, and they looked to me as an example. I couldn't ask my friends, because personal financial issues just weren't something we talked about on a regular basis. It felt good to drive a nice car and be able to show that we had money. But I wasn't about to tell my best friend that Jennifer and I had been living month to month for the past year, at a time when we were making more than we ever had before.

By Wednesday of the new week, I was looking forward to the meeting with Aunt Katherine, and I pulled into the restaurant 15 minutes early. I was going to pay the waitress ahead of time for lunch and surprise Aunt Katherine, but when I walked inside, I saw her, already settled into our booth.

"Hello, Michael!" she said cheerfully. "How is your week going? Did you get your homework completed?"

I smiled. "Yes, I did. I made a long list. Jen and I sat down and worked on it together."

"I'm impressed!" she said.

"Me too. We're pretty busy these days. . . . in fact, Jen was going to join us, but she got caught up in a special project at school."

"How are the kids?"

"Oh they're great. Expensive, but great."

"It's just the beginning, Mike. Wait until they get into the teen years! Things like clothes, laptops, field trips. Soon they'll need a lot more than simple toys!"

I nodded but said nothing. Those were the things I didn't want to think about right now.

"I've been thinking a lot about our lunch last week," I said. "I have to admit I'm taking financial matters a lot more seriously now."

"Really?"

"Yes, but I'm also kind of at a roadblock. I feel so overwhelmed and confused when I start thinking about our financial situation."

"You sound the same way you did at our first lunch meeting, Mike. Overwhelmed. Too many questions and not enough answers."

"Yes. That's it. And I have to admit, I want your advice. I really do, Aunt Kath ... and don't take this the wrong way ... " I hesitated. I wasn't really certain how to say it. "But I'm not sure you're helping me," I blurted.

"Well, Michael, I'm probably not."

I stared at her blankly, waiting for the punch line. It was not funny.

"It's up to you to help yourself," she said finally.

"Well, then, I'm confused. Why are we talking about this at all these weekly meetings. I thought we'd talk about investments and what you and Uncle George did. I want to know your secret."

Aunt Katherine laughed. "Oh, I see," she said. "You want to know the *secret*."

"Yes," I said defensively. "The secret to building wealth." I didn't want to talk about feelings and beliefs and all that mumbo jumbo. "Don't get me wrong, but I'm a numbers guy. I wanted to talk about your secret. The investments you made, the stocks you picked. Not things to think about, like beliefs, attitudes, or feelings."

"Most people want the secret. They want to rush to the finish line and discover the magic bullet to success! But there's no magic bullet, Mike. There is no *secret*. This is a long race. It's a marathon, not a sprint. If

*There is no secret.*

*This is a long race.*

*Your financial journey is a marathon,*

*not a sprint.*

you're not willing to learn how to make it to the finish line, you just won't. There's no other way to say it. I'm not a money manager, Michael. Like I said before, it's these elements of behavior—the things we've been talking about—that will go a long way in determining your financial success."

"Okay, okay. Fine. We can talk about knowledge, beliefs, whatever you want. But I wanted to talk about money."

"We are talking about money. Everything we do affects the way we earn money, save money, and spend money. Everything we believe and feel affects the way we act. Those behaviors, the way we act, the things we do, affect our financial future. Got it?"

"I think so."

"So let's talk about the things you believe to be true. That's a good place to start."

I looked down at my list.

Our Financial Beliefs

   He who dies with the most toys wins

   You need credit cards to build
   credit

   Saving for college is important
   (for the kids)

   You save too much for college and
   your kids won't be eligible for loans

   The key to a successful financial
   future is picking the right
   investments

   The government will take care of
   my future

   Money can't buy happiness
   (but it can!)

Aunt Katherine read the list. "So these are your beliefs?"

I nodded. "Jen and I did it together at the breakfast table one morning."

"I see we've got some work to do."

"That bad?"

"Well, not bad, certainly, but I see you both have bought into some misconceptions about the key to a successful financial future. For one thing, picking the right investments is certainly important to building wealth, but there are a few basics that are much more important to long-term wealth accumulation. The right investments are just one part of it."

I leaned back, skeptical. "How so?"

"Well, long ago, I learned that there are three variables that impact wealth accumulation: time, rate of return, and the amount invested. Time, in my view, is the most important element that affects the size of your estate. So, it's not just about picking the right investments. That alone can't make you financially successful. It's about making sure you plan and think about all three variables . . . and don't forget

*There are three variables*
*that impact wealth accumulation:*
*time,*
*rate of return,*
*and amount invested.*
*Time has the greatest impact*
*on the outcome*
*of your investments.*

about the adverse impact that procrastination can have on your long-term financial success. It is relatively simple, but at the same time difficult to do.

"Michael, we've talked last week and today about what you know or believe about financial matters. This morning I was reading an article on investing that had an example of the power of time in investing that might help reinforce that aspect of what we've been talking about. Here's the article, why don't you review it while I go and say hello to my friend, Marsha, who just walked in."

I read the article and made a few notes while Aunt Katherine talked with her friend. The numbers were astonishing.

Assume two people have 30 years to invest.

Person #1 gets started right away by putting $3,000 a year in an investment that notionally earns 10%/year and invests for 8 years and then stops investing but leaves the money where it is earning 10% (that person has invested $24,000).

Person #2 delays starting to save to buy some "essentials" like a sports car and doesn't start investing until person #1 stops. Person #2 invests $3,000/year for the next 22 years at the same 10%/year return (invests a total of $66,000)

Which person will have more money after 30 years?

Person # 1 will have $307, 201
Person #2 will have $235,629
Person # 1 invests less, ends up with more!

Aunt Katherine returned. "So what do you think?" she asked.

"Now you're speaking my language. I took a stocks class in college, and I was the star of the class. I earned more than anyone else in the investing contest."

"So investing comes naturally to you?"

"It's one of my skills, I like to think."

"What investments do you have?"

"Well, none at the moment, other than my company stock program. But I plan to."

"Well, as I said before, time is a key element, so you need to move from 'planning' to action. The key is getting started—to save and invest early—and take full advantage of the power of compound interest."

Uncle George's round TO IT flashed into my mind again!

"Oh yeah, 401(k) and all that. We do that. I give 2 percent at work and they match it."

"But you could be contributing more and leveraging your company's contribution."

"We just can't afford it right now," I said.

Aunt Katherine shook her head. "You can't afford *not* to, Michael. That's free money your company is willing to contribute, and you're leaving it on the table."

I stared at her. Maybe we could cut back on the lawn service. Maybe there were other things we could cut back on. She was right.

"Look," she said. "Investing isn't rocket science. It requires some planning and the involvement of an expert can be very helpful. But the basics are easy enough for you to do to get started."

"Like focusing on the basics of what we believe, what we feel, what we think, and so on?"

"Yes, exactly. The key is rooted in behavior and the elements that influence behavior. These are the elements we've been focusing on." She looked at the list. "Which brings me to this next point. You wrote, 'the government will take care of my future.' Do you really believe that?"

"I don't, but Jen does. She wrote it. She was talking about Social Security."

"But at least, right now, I don't think I would consider Social Security as a guarantee for someone your age, Michael. The government can only do so much to protect you and Jen, and at best, your Social Security checks would be merely a subsistence income . . . certainly not enough to classify as a 'successful financial future.' Counting on the government for anything beyond the basics is unrealistic."

I sat back and let out a deep breath. My throat felt dry, and I took a sip of water.

"Are you okay?"

I shook my head.

"It's okay, Michael. You're young. You still have a lot of time to plan and to execute! The principles we're talking about can change people's lives even if they're much older than you are. So they can help you and Jennifer."

"So what's my next step?"

"Next week we'll talk about values. Think about it, Michael. Think about the values you were raised with and how they affect your thoughts about money. I'll see you next week."

Aunt Katherine was gone in a flash. This was getting harder than I thought.

## Beliefs

Beliefs strongly shape our behavior . . .
if the belief is faulty, guess what?
Our behavior will be misguided.

There are a lot of "financial beliefs"
out there that just aren't true:

We DON'T need a lot of credit
cards to build good credit.

Picking the right investments is NOT
the most important element of a
successful financial future.

Paying the minimum on our credit
card debt is NOT OK.

We need to be thoughtful when
being guided by what we consider
financial "truths" and habits.

There seems to be a lot to know
regarding the truths about a sound
financial program ... how can we be
sure that we know all that we need
to know? (I'm starting to understand
why Aunt Kath uses a financial
advisor.)

Becoming very clear that TIME
is a huge element in the pursuit
of long-term financial success ...
procrastination HURTS!

# FIVE

# Values

J ENNIFER AND I ARRIVED at the restaurant a few minutes late for our lunch meeting. Aunt Katherine was
waiting in the booth, her salad already ordered and on the
table in front of her. Jennifer and I ordered, anxious to get
down to business.

"It's been a hard week," I admitted, taking a bite. "I've
hardly been able to sleep, thinking about all of this."

"But I see it hasn't affected your appetite!"

I laughed. "Very funny."

"What's keeping you up at night, son?"

"I just feel like I've taken a huge step backward since
our first meeting."

Aunt Katherine just stared at me quietly. I took another bite of my cheeseburger. "I went back and reviewed our notes from the last few lunches. So far we've talked about knowledge, attitudes, truths, beliefs, and now values. I just don't feel like we're getting anywhere. I feel like a hamster on a treadmill, just running in place."

"Because you wanted to talk about stocks."

"Well, not just stocks, but annuities, investments, bonds, all that stuff. That's what gets me excited. That's the kind of stuff I'm ready to dive right into to start building wealth."

"Do you feel the same way?" she asked Jennifer.

"No, I like these discussions!"

"If you want to talk specifics about stocks and bonds, Michael, you need to talk to a financial professional. But you asked me about my secret, and I'm telling you that there's no one magic bullet. These elements of behavior that we're talking about are the *real* secrets to building financial success."

"How do you know?" I asked.

"I learned them, just like you're learning them now."

"From whom?"

"Well, from George, for one. But he learned it from our financial advisor."

I sat for a while and pulled out my list. "I'm not the most patient person, if you haven't figured that out yet," I said, smiling.

Aunt Katherine watched as I read through my list on values. "I looked up the word *values* in the dictionary," I said. "Thought that was a good place to start."

"And what did you find?"

"Values especially of a traditional or conservative kind that are held to promote the sound functioning of the family and to strengthen the fabric of society."

"So does that help you with what we'll be talking about today?" she asked.

"Not really. Let me read you the definition I found online, in Wikipedia."

"Wiki-what?"

"It's an online dictionary. The definitions are much different than Webster's. They usually offer a lot more. In Wikipedia, values are defined as:

Each individual has certain underlying **values** that contribute to their value system. Integrity in the application of a "value" ensures its continuity and this continuity separates a value from beliefs, opinion and ideas.

I sat back in the booth. "That one got me thinking."

"Really, how so?"

"It got me thinking about integrity. And the last part of that definition says that values are separate from beliefs, opinions, and ideas. I found that interesting. Before, I thought they were all the same. But it's the integrity thing that's got me thinking, because I don't think I've been totally honest with you."

Aunt Katherine seemed unruffled by my admission. She took a bite of her salad and delicately rested her fork on the side of her plate. She dabbed her mouth with the paper napkin and looked at me inquisitively.

"Integrity means honesty, and maybe I haven't been totally honest with myself or with you."

"What do you mean, Michael?"

Jennifer shifted in her seat.

"Well, my only goal coming into this, I have to admit, was to find out how you made all your money. See, I've seen you and Uncle George through the years, taking all of those trips, living so well, and how different your family was from ours. We always lived in the smallest homes and the mediocre neighborhoods. We couldn't always afford the right clothes, things like that. I wanted to know what you did differently than my parents and other people I knew. But in the back of my mind, I've had a different goal that I never shared with you."

"Which was?"

"Well, I really didn't think about it until this week, when I started thinking about my values. I guess I had pushed it to the back of my mind. But when I first contacted you to talk about this, my goal was heavy in the forefront of my mind." I looked down at the few bites that were left of the burger. "It's been my goal to be a millionaire by age thirty."

Aunt Katherine leaned back. "So, you want to be a millionaire by age thirty?"

"Yes. It's been my goal since I was a kid working a paper route."

"Well, that's a common dream, Michael. You might be surprised to learn that a large number of people have that thought. Then 30 passes, and, well . . ."

"Aunt Kath, why do you call it a dream or thought, not a goal?" I asked.

"Michael, a goal is bound up by a realistic plan and behavior. Remember that word?" she responded.

"Well, I'm going to do it!" I countered.

"That's only a few years, Michael," she said.

Jennifer patted me on the back.

"I know, but some people hit it big, invent things, become entrepreneurs. Maybe I can start a business."

"It took us years to hit that mark, Michael. And there wasn't any magic bullet. We achieved it with all of the things you and I are focusing on now. By changing our behavior and focusing on values." Aunt Katherine leaned forward. "Tell me something. Why is it important for you to hit that millionaire mark? How will your life change?"

"Are you kidding? Everything will change!"

"What will change?"

"I'll have freedom, for one. I won't have to punch the clock or report to anyone else. I'll be able to do what I want."

"Having a million dollars doesn't mean you'll be able to stop working. There are still bills to pay, and chances are, you'd raise your standard of living. Your mortgage would be higher. Your living costs would be higher. You still have college to pay for, and by the time your kids are grown, that could cost $50,000 to $100,000 dollars for each one, per year, depending on the school they go to!"

I sat and thought about what she said. I still wanted to be a millionaire.

"Look, becoming a millionaire isn't a bad goal. But you have to think about the values behind that goal. What about that goal is really, truly important to you? Is it the freedom money will buy? Because it all sounds very self-centered. So far you're talking about what that goal will get you. But what will it get your family?"

"I'm sure Jennifer wouldn't mind being a millionairess," I laughed. Jennifer smiled.

"Again, Michael, it's noble to have ambition and goals. Better than having none at all. But becoming a millionaire—what does that mean? It means you have more money in the bank than you do now, but does it mean that you have a better life? You should examine your values. What drives your desire to be a millionaire? What is it that's important about that?"

"The freedom, for one. The freedom to be my own boss. But I guess I'd need my own company for that, which would mean a complete change of lifestyle. I'd have to find something that I could do, maybe a product or service. And then that would probably take more time away from my kids ..."

"But you don't have to be your own boss to become a millionaire. There are a lot of people who have saved for years and invested the right way who have achieved that goal. Like George and me."

"I guess money isn't the end-all," I said. "It's just a means to an end. I don't want to feel like a worker bee in a cubicle for the rest of my life. Right now I feel like just a number."

"Money is just a method to achieving your dreams. Money isn't the ultimate goal. It's just a method to fund your dreams and your lifestyle."

"I think I'm starting to get it now. I guess I don't have to become Donald Trump by the time I'm thirty."

"If you make the right choices, you might just earn and save more than a million dollars. But I think you should spend some time thinking about your values some more. What's truly important to you. So far you haven't mentioned any of the things that I suspect are really important to you."

"Like what?"

"Well, like the kids, for one. I'm sure you'll want to put them in the best college, if I know you. I'm sure that's important. And I know you want to spend time with them. So having freedom to do that is important."

"I want to take them to Washington, D.C. and to the Grand Canyon. I want to take them places I never went as a kid, to teach them about our country, show them the beautiful landmarks. That takes money."

"And if those trips are important to you, you'll have to budget and plan for them. Which means making smart, value-oriented financial decisions. So, for instance, when it's time to upgrade that stainless-steel grill out back for the newest model the neighbors just bought, you'll be able to think about whether that grill is more important to you than the trip to the Grand Canyon with the kids."

"The trip, for sure, is more important. But I see where you're going with all of this now. If we have our values in mind, rather than just the things we want, we'll be in a better position to make financial choices, and we won't react based on our emotions. So maybe if I set goals, I mean, if *we* sit down tonight, Jennifer and I, and set goals, we will both have the same mind-set."

"Exactly, you can have a family meeting over dinner. George and I always did that."

"I like that idea," Jennifer said.

"Goals based on your values," Aunt Katherine said. "That's your homework."

## Values

Money is not the only component of a successful future.

Money is important, but what in life is more important than money to us?

Money facilitates those values that are really important ... freedom, supporting my family, leaving a legacy, etc.

What are Jennifer and my values and how does financial success play in those values?

What is really important to us ... not unlike "needs" and "wants".

SIX

# Goals

JENNIFER AND I MET Aunt Katherine at the restaurant, and she looked ten years younger than she had the week before. Her smile was radiant, and she bounced in full of energy!

"Hi, kids," she said, beaming. "Did you have a great week?"

"Yes, actually. We did." I felt my energy level increasing just by being with her. "I thought about our discussion, and I've been looking forward to this week."

"Today we're going to talk goals!" she said, smiling. "It's exciting, because now I feel like we're at a stage where you're ready to move forward and set some goals for your financial future."

"Jennifer and I had a great discussion about this last week. We actually made a list of all of the things we wanted. We both had different goals, of course, but some were the same.

"We got a baby-sitter and went to dinner and brought our notepads with us. We talked about values and misconceptions and attitudes about money," Jennifer added.

"How did you feel about that meeting?"

"Great!" Jennifer said. "In fact, it was so successful that we decided to add a financial date night to our schedule, once a month. We'll go to the same restaurant, bring our notepads. No kids."

"Does talking about money make for a disagreeable date?" she smiled.

"Well, it gets heated at times," I said. "But we set some ground rules. We agreed not to get mad. Just to listen to the other person's point of view and to agree to disagree."

"Those are good rules. I'm proud of you two."

"This is fun, Aunt Katherine. Financial issues aren't something we ignore now. Because of you and these mentoring meetings, it's all out in the open. It's no longer the big elephant in the room that no one understands."

"Isn't it refreshing to be different from your friends?"

"It's great," Jennifer said. "Personal financial issues aren't something anyone talks about in our circle of friends, because everyone *acts* like they've got a lot of money. Even our friends who don't have steady jobs seem to have the best of everything and spend a lot of money. But we are going to live differently now. We're going to address everything and think about our values and behaviors."

"It takes discipline, but it's worth it in the end," said Aunt Katherine. "And I'm so glad to see your enthusiasm. So let's talk about goals. Setting goals is the first step to realizing your dreams. Without goals life, including the financial aspect, very often devolves into aimless wandering."

I thought about that for a moment. She certainly did seem wise.

"Jen and I have done reasonably well, but a lot of it has been aimless wandering. We make decisions spur of the moment, for instance, based on emotions. Decisions like going to the national championship game when we didn't have the money. We paid six hundred dollars just for the game tickets, and then there was the airfare and hotel. That was a fun weekend, but it set us back two thousand dollars, and we could have watched it on television. With what you've gotten me to think about, I compounded that two-thousand-dollar trip over twenty years, and even if it earned just a reasonable 8 percent, we could have had over ninety-three hundred dollars available for the kids' college or some other more important goal."

"There are a few things about goals that are important to know and understand," Aunt Katherine said. "Goals need to be specific, measurable, understandable, and achievable. Goals put a 'stake in the ground' toward which to navigate in your life ... both near and on the horizon. It's easy to see the ones closer in. But the goals on the horizon help guide you to your value-driven vision for your life. Those are the ones that are really important, even though they're harder to see."

"So how do we start setting those?" Jennifer asked.

"They're values based, so it's easier than you think. Your goals come from the things that are really important to you, what you want your life to stand for. Remember all our discussions about values, and what you and Jennifer really want for yourselves and for the kids? Everyone has different values. Your goals should not just be plucked out of thin air. They should be developed. When they are, they will be based on and support what you value in life and what is important to you . . . both in the near term and in the future."

"I see. How long will it take?"

"The process of discovering the values that drive your life and your goals requires some introspection . . . and not just solitary time. So that's a hard one to answer. She sat back in the booth and smiled. "Often the short-term goals will lead to longer-term goals, but they can also stand on their own . . . as long as they are driven by your values."

"That actually sounds like fun. We're halfway there, since we talked a lot about this on our date night. A surprise discovery for both of us is that we now know each other better. We talked about what we want for the kids, college, travel, and things like that. But how do we know if we've set the right goals?"

"They have to feel authentic. Your goals are right when they reflect the realistic things you value in your life." She paused and took a sip of her water. "And you also have to think about adding in measurable milestones along the way to your goals—for longer-term goals you need 'how am I doing' milestones along the way to ensure that you stay on track toward your goals."

"Really?" Jennifer asked.

"Yes. And often, short-term goals provide those milestones. But your budget helps put everything in the right perspective."

"That's been the hardest thing for us to agree on. A budget."

"It usually is. But even if you can get a rough draft on paper, it helps to put your goals in the right perspective, because it helps you to set goals based on reality."

I leaned back and made some notes.

"We've got a lot to do this week, Aunt Katherine."

"Yes, you do."

"But I'm fired up about it!"

"Good. You and Jennifer can reach much of what you dream of. But in order for that to happen, you'll need to start with what you want. What you *really* want. For now and for 50 years from now. Those are the things you can talk about with a financial advisor. George and I did."

"Did he tell you what characteristics wealthy people share? I'd like to know. You know, their traits and habits."

"Ah, yes." She smiled.

I waited.

"Well, there are many, but three primary behaviors are discipline, long-term commitment to a financial plan, and realistic and achievable goals."

I nodded. "Sounds pretty simple."

"Basically, from a values perspective, financial success requires the discipline to live within your means and pay yourself first, a commitment to your financial goals, and the sense to develop an efficient plan to get you there. To do this in the most effective way possible, you have to know your values. You have to know what's important to you."

"So how should we go about discovering our values?" I asked.

She smiled. "Well, everything stems from what's important to you. You have to set specific goals that are in line with and supported by your personal values and beliefs. It's more of a holistic approach. I think that sitting down with someone would be good—when you're ready."

"Do you think I'm ready?"

"I don't know, Michael. It sure can't hurt. I'm not a professional. I'm just giving you information that I've learned over time, either through experience or from our advisor."

I checked my watch. "I hate to cut our meeting short this week, but I have a big client meeting to prepare for."

Aunt Katherine smiled. "Go ahead, Michael. I'll see you next week, same time, same place. Jennifer and I can finish up!"

"What's our homework?"

"Patience," she said.

"Patience?"

"Yes. Patience and discipline. That's what we're going to talk about. So, no homework for you, except to think about those two things."

"Okay." I pecked them both on the cheek and left in a flash.

## Goals

Goals—help guide behavior

Goals put a "stake in the ground" toward which to navigate in life ... both near and on the horizon.

Developing meaningful goals for our financial life will take work ... and they will need to be periodically reviewed and updated.

Values based-goals should not be "plucked out of thin air" they should be developed. Properly developed, they will be based on what we value in life.

Goals characteristics: specific, measurable, understandable, achievable

Without goals, life (including the financial aspect) very often will be nothing more than aimless wandering.

A budget helps put goals in proper perspective (reality).

# SEVEN

# Patience & Discipline

I SAT SILENT FOR A while. For the first ten minutes of our meeting, we ordered, finished our food, and spent the entire time talking about the kids. I suspected Aunt Katherine was giving me time to digest before she came up with the hard questions. We both knew this was my hardest behavior, or trait, to think about. Patient was the last thing I was. As a competitive athlete throughout my years in college, patience was the last thing I needed. I was aggressive, fast, and focused on being that way in my career as well. I believed that the early bird got the worm. After all, life is short. How could patience be an asset? Finally, Aunt Katherine looked at me. She asked me a question.

"What do you think of, when you think of the word *patience*?"

I sat silently, mulling an answer. I counted silently to ten in an attempt to be *patient*.

"It's not a positive word," I blurted. "It's a slow word. Patience, slow, the turtle. Second place. I guess I'm geared to the opposite. I'm young, Aunt Katherine! Carpe diem, just do it, seize the moment, and all that! I want to achieve our goals now. I want to buy a new house someday soon, maybe get a sports car. You only live once."

She laughed. "Okay ..."

"C'mon, what about patience is fun?"

"Patience isn't about fun, Michael, but it can be a very valuable trait. You think the world's great warriors didn't have patience? I suspect that many victories have come about because a leader patiently assessed the enemy's strengths and weaknesses.

Jennifer and I sat and listened.

"You can still seize opportunities and be a patient person. Lots of great leaders are patient. Patience isn't a weakness, it's a strength. Especially when it comes to financial success. Think of patience as aggressively choosing the right thing."

"But if you're too patient, you can miss great investments, stock opportunities," I said.

"Oh, that's a dangerous belief, and it's a misconception. You might be able to hit a good stock on its way up once in a while, Michael. But if you're not a financial professional who does that for a living, you're just a gambler."

I nodded. I had lost money on "sure things" from the advice of friends.

"Patience is not his best trait," Jennifer said.

"Remember back when you played sports, Michael?" asked Aunt Katherine.

"Yes. All through high school and college. I was captain of my soccer team in college."

"The qualities you had to have in sports are similar to the qualities you have to have now as a leader of your family and as a big part of your financial future for your family. You play a big role on the team, and you have to have the right traits in order to win the game."

"Well, quickness and prowess and cunning were always important in sports."

"Explain that."

"If you weren't quick, Aunt Katherine, you wouldn't maintain possession of the ball. The opposing team would steal it from you."

She nodded. "Okay, so was the quickest player on the team the best player?"

I shook my head and said, "No."

"Why not?"

"Well, one of our top players was really, really quick, but he couldn't always score a goal because sometimes he was too quick. He would move down the field faster than the other team, but he was so fast he went faster than our players, too. They couldn't get him to pass the ball, so they couldn't help him score a goal."

"So what would happen?"

"He'd try to make all the goals himself," I said. It dawned on me what she was alluding to. "So you're saying I need to be part of a team . . . not make all the goals by myself."

"Well, soccer isn't a solitary sport," she said. "You don't go out there on the field by yourself, and you don't play against yourself. You have a team that assists you down the field, into the goal. You have players you pass to. Some have quickness and agility. Others are patient. They can develop a strategy in their minds, always planning, but waiting for just the right moment to kick or pass the ball and help you win."

"And the best players have both," I said. "Because the entire team is important; the players leverage off each other to win."

"That's right, Michael. Now you get it. Financial planning is just like a sports competition. You have to have patience, among other qualities, to be a winner."

"Other qualities like what?" Jennifer asked.

"Like discipline."

"Because the path to a successful financial future is a marathon, not a sprint," I said, smiling.

Aunt Katherine laughed. "That's right! And also because time is the key component in asset accumulation."

I leaned forward. "Go on."

"If you don't have the patience and discipline to wait for time and compounding to grow your assets, you won't be able to establish real wealth. Winners stay focused on personal behavior over time rather than short-term results. It's the same way in athletics, Michael. You think Tiger Woods only focuses on his golf match that week?"

I shook my head. "No, he trains every day. All year. I read somewhere that he trains mentally and physically, up to seven hours a day. And it's not just practicing golf. He trains his mind, meditates, and cross-trains by working out. In fact, I would guess that virtually all the top athletes have personal coaches."

"See, maybe it's time you and Jennifer do a bit of cross-training. To win, you'll need to start finding ways to incorporate patience and discipline into your lives each and every day, to start building up those skills and habits. Maybe you can make a list of two or three things you can do every day that require patience and discipline."

"Like listening to the kids more. That requires patience," I said with a laugh.

Aunt Katherine smiled. "Sure, we could all listen more, and better. But you could also focus on two money behaviors every day. The first is paying yourself first. Set aside a little for savings every payday, don't wait to see what is left over. The second is spending less than you make. You can try to search for areas to spend less in every day. You'd be amazed how one less coffee or deli sandwich a week can add up."

"What else can we do?" Jennifer asked.

"Be patient," she said. "And disciplined. Your financial future will improve. Start allocating a portion of each raise to your financial future by increasing your savings. That takes patience and discipline, because you'll want to buy things for the kids or the house. Also, understand and constantly remind yourselves that you are committed to your long-term goals . . . don't be distracted by short-term issues such as market fluctuations. Keep your focus on the future."

"And there's always a way to justify it, you know, carpe diem, you only live once," said Michael with a laugh.

"Sure, I know. And we do only live once here on earth. But you can choose to live financially secure or choose to live struggling, living from month to month. You don't want to create that legacy for your kids."

"No, and I won't. I'm going to do it, Aunt Katherine. I'm a believer, and I know I need patience. With Jennifer's help, we're going to build true wealth. The kind that lasts."

I left the restaurant with a lot more enthusiasm and anxiety than we had going in, but also with a strange sense of peace.

## Patience and Discipline

Patience and discipline—two more elements that affect behavior

Achieving financial success and security is a marathon, not a sprint. (unless I can win the lottery ... and then make wise decisions thereafter!)

Time is the key component in building wealth ... _being patient_ over long periods of time by remaining focused on our value-driven goals.

We have to have the discipline to "pay ourselves first" ... we need to spend less than we earn.

## EIGHT

# The Plan

I WAS SO ANXIOUS TO get to the restaurant, I parked as fast as I could and sprinted to the front door. Aunt Katherine was sitting at the table, waiting for me, as always, and our lunch was already there, too. After a few minutes, Jennifer joined us on her lunch break from school.

We all huddled together. "We wrote out our goals," I said right away. "We did it! I feel so much better."

Aunt Katherine smiled. "Sounds like you're having fun now."

"We are! And we're ready for the next step." I pushed our goal sheet across the table. "Take it home and look at it. See if there's anything I'm missing."

Aunt Katherine looked down. "It seems like you covered a lot," she said. "There are two full pages here!"

I nodded. It had taken us several hours, but it was fun to dream, to talk about the second vacation home we'd have, once the kids were off to college.

"The budget was a dose of reality though," Jennifer said.

"It's easy to dream, isn't it?"

I nodded. "Yeah, but that's all it is without the resources. Just a dream." I winked at Aunt Kath, "Goals are bound up by behavior."

"This is great. Michael, we've talked about the role behavior plays in financial success and what traits can affect behavior. Now it's time to talk about something that can tie those traits into positive behavior. George and I were always rediscovering how beneficial a basic plan could be in helping us to get to where we wanted to go. You've got the goals, and now you and Jennifer have to have a plan to make sure those goals come to fruition. You have to have a plan to reach your goals. Have you thought about that?"

"No," I admitted. "That one had us tied up in knots. It seems like there's so much we want that we'll never have enough money for it. Unless we spend on credit."

"But credit is a burden," Jennifer said.

"That's right," said Aunt Katherine.

"I know. We won't do that. We value the freedom that financial success will give us more than anything. And we're ready to do the hard work to become successful. Like having the discipline it will take to achieve our goals. And the patience. Jennifer is better at that than I am."

"But you have some real strengths as part of your team," she said. "Like your ability to sell and earn money and make a good financial plan."

"Thanks, Aunt Katherine."

"And every year, he gets promoted," Jennifer said. "He's got a great career going!"

"That's good," Aunt Katherine said. "But you also need a financial plan to help guide your behavior."

"How so? I mean, I know we need one. But how will it help us change the way we act and think about spending and about needing versus wanting?"

"Well," she said, "George learned early on in his flying career of the critical need to plan. He had the airplane, he had the fuel, he had in mind where he wanted to end up ... but what he needed to tie all those together was a flight plan ... a structured, methodical way to take the resources he had and use them to reach a destination. Planning also helped make the decisions required during the flight much easier."

I made a note on the margin of my page. *You can't reach your destination without a plan.* I had read it many times before in various books and articles. It certainly seemed to be true, but I never really applied it to our financial future.

"That's the essence of planning ... using resources in an organized way to achieve a desired goal. And of course, planning is critical to successful military operations, but I think you'll see how important it is in day-to-day life. Once you and Jennifer start thinking about what influences your behavior—the things like attitude, knowledge, beliefs, values, goals, patience, and discipline—you'll be able to see how you can tie all those elements together in a way that will help guide your personal behavior. I guess the best way to put it is that going through life without some form of a plan virtually guarantees that you won't reach your full potential."

I sat back in the chair. "Wow."

"I know that sounds harsh. But think about it. You said your goal was to be a millionaire by 30, but that goal won't be reached because you don't have a plan on how to do it. Not that this particular goal is realistic, mind you," she smiled.

"But I thought I'd hit a get-rich-quick scheme somewhere along the way!"

She laughed. "Yeah, most kids do. But, Michael, hope is not a plan, and life without a plan will likely become a series of aimless journeys with, at best, short-term objectives that have little or no relationship to what you really value. See, you've been great at knowing what you want, but maybe not so great at the big picture of setting goals, determining how your values and behaviors affect those goals, and knowing what your ultimate objective is."

I grabbed my pen and pulled out a sheet of paper. "I'm ready. Tell me where to start!" Jennifer just smiled.

"Okay. Let's talk about the elements of a plan. The word *planning* can sound ominous, especially for someone like you who likes results. But, in fact, a plan—written or 'in one's head'—is made of just a few basic elements. It's not ominous at all."

"What are they?" I was prepared to write them down.

"The first element is core or personal values. This makes up who you are, what you believe. The second is a vision for your personal future—"

"You mean, our plan?"

"Well, the vision comes before your plan, but it's certainly a part of it."

"How do we define our vision?"

"Well," she said, looking into my eyes. "How do you want to define yourself 'when you grow up'?"

"When I grow up, I want to be rich and free."

"And what will that get you?"

"Rich means *security* to me. Free to spend time with my family and to have enough money to buy them what they want and need. Based on the goals that come from our personal values, of course."

"And what about you, Jennifer?"

"Well, one thing we know is that we want to pay for all four years of college for each child. So that's a goal, I suppose."

"So to achieve that important goal, your strategy could include opening some sort of college investment account in each child's name."

"Like a 529 plan?" I said.

"Maybe," she said. "A good financial advisor can tell you the pros and cons and guide you to the right tool to use to reach your goal. But no one can set your goals for you."

I made some notes. Jennifer took a deep breath.

"Next, you have to think of the specific activities you and Jennifer will undertake to implement your strategies.

For instance, regarding your goal of helping your children attend college, will you set aside a hundred dollars each paycheck to invest in the children's college fund?"

"Yes, we plan to."

"You'll have to develop strategies for every goal."

"I see."

"And you'll have to decide on the activities to which you will commit to make the strategy work."

"Next, you want to think about the intermediate objectives or other measures of success. For instance, by the time your children are eight, what will the investment account need to have in it for you to be on track? That's just an example, mind you. I don't know exactly what it needs to be to keep up with the rate of inflation and all the other variables."

"This is great stuff, Aunt Katherine. Go on."

"I think you get the picture. You'll need to develop a solid plan for your future. You're on the right track now. A plan helps keep all of life in balance. We live in a complex world, Michael. It's difficult to see how life in that world can be kept in balance without thoughtful consideration or a plan."

"I know. There's just too much temptation. Even driving here, I saw a new car I've been eying for a long time. But according to our plan, if I bought that sports car, we wouldn't be able to take another vacation for five years!" I laughed. "Well, I might be exaggerating, but it would cut some of our goals short. Like college, for instance."

"There will be temptations all along the way, Michael and Jennifer. You'll have to make sure your plan includes personal accountability to follow it. A financial advisor can help with that."

"I'm excited now."

"You'll want to continually update your plan and its elements. I won't be around to guide you forever, and you'll have to stick with it. Life is not static, and although planning does take some time, it cannot be considered an end-all ... things will change, tomorrow will be different than planned." Her voice trailed off. I sensed that she was thinking about Uncle George. "But changes in life aren't a good excuse to abandon your personal plan. I'm still sticking to ours today and enjoying the benefits."

"And I want to have a plan my family can rely on," I said. "No matter what happens."

"Me too," Jennifer added.

Aunt Katherine smiled. "Good plan, kids. Your future will be secure!"

## Planning

The elements of a plan are:

Values—who are we? What do we value? Why?

Vision—where are we ultimately going? How do we want to define ourselves?

Goals—what substantive things do we want to achieve that will lead to our vision?

Strategies—what will we do in a broad sense to achieve our goals?

Activities—what will we do on a daily and continuing basis to implement our strategies?

Objectives—what intermediate goals will help measure the progress with our plan?

ACCOUNTABILITY—a plan is just so much fluff unless we follow the plan and keep it updated as our circumstances change—it's our plan!

Planning helps bring order to life situations amidst challenge, confusion, and change.

# NINE

# A Financial Planning Model

J ENNIFER AND I DROVE to the restaurant for the last meeting with Aunt Katherine. Snow began to fall on the windshield, the snowflakes touching and then melting quickly. I thought about the seasons in Colorado and how they seemed to change so quickly, just like the different seasons of our lives. Just a few years ago, we were in college ourselves, then the wedding, the births of our kids, and soon we'll be sending them off to college, too. The seasons continually changed.

We found Aunt Katherine in the same booth as always.

"Good afternoon!" she said, smiling. "Isn't this snow beautiful?"

"It sure is," I said. I looked down to my notes. "I'm so excited about our plan," I said. "We sat down and talked and created it. Jennifer and I are now officially on the same page," I said, smiling. "Only one problem."

"What's that?" she asked.

"We don't know where to go from here."

Jennifer smiled. "That's right."

"Well, a good financial planning model has three fundamental, key elements that a financial advisor can help you develop. You'll need to sit down with someone who can guide you and Jennifer along the way."

"What are the three elements?"

"That's something your financial advisor can share with you. He or she will cover everything once you sit down to talk about your goals. I can tell you, but you'd just be getting information second-hand."

"I'm definitely going to call an advisor, but I want you to tell me. What are the three elements?"

"Well, I know for sure that a good financial planning model includes things like managing risk, managing income and liquid savings, and asset accumulation and management. These are the things George and I always talked about with our advisor. These are the three areas you'll want to think about your entire life."

"So it sounds pretty simple. Maybe I was making it too hard."

"It can be simple," she said. "Once you learn the basics from an expert."

"Tell me more about those three elements." I wanted to know more.

"I love your enthusiasm," she said. "Risk management is about insurance, Michael. Because most people have a poor understanding of the various forms of insurance out there."

"We don't have any right now, but I know we need it."

Aunt Katherine nodded. "Yes, you do. But your advisor can tell you exactly what to get, based on your family goals and needs. Most people overly focus on the 'money' side of a financial plan versus the 'risk-management' side, because investing is much more glamorous than insurance."

"I agree!"

"But if you skimp on key elements of insurance like life insurance, protecting your property, protecting your earnings if you should become disabled, it could be disastrous for your family."

I thought about Jennifer and the kids. I wanted to make sure they were protected. For life.

"And what's the basic premise of the cash-management aspect?" Jennifer asked. "Savings?"

"Yes, cash management is about allocating your income between your spending plan and savings, but it's also about an emergency fund and a liquid savings account to help you with managing and avoiding debt. Like the excessive use of credit cards, which can sabotage your financial future and eat into what you can save."

I nodded. We had our share. But all that was about to stop. We had a better plan now.

"The last aspect of the financial planning model is asset accumulation and management. That's the fun part for you, because you like investments. So that will include

---

understanding your investment opportunities and things like time, amount of input, and rate of return."

"Lots to learn, Aunt Katherine. I wish we would have started this five years ago."

"But you're starting now," she said. "And that's great! You are giving yourself the opportunity to not be saying the same thing five years from now."

The waitress came by, and I paid the check before Aunt Katherine had a chance to reach for her purse. This week, I was prepared.

"Thank you, Michael." She leaned over and hugged both of us.

"Thank you," I said. "This could just be the best investment I ever made."

"The time you and Jen spend planning for your financial future as well as successfully following your plan will be one of the best investments you will ever make," she said. And as we parted, and I left the restaurant thinking about our future. I knew she was right.

What have I learned?

1. My personal behavior has a big impact on our financial future.

2. Our financial behavior is affected by:

Our _Attitude_ about financial matters.

Our _Knowledge_ about financial matters (or _the lack of it_).

Our _Beliefs_ (beliefs can be wrong and misguided).

Our _Values_ (what is really important to us ... what guides us?).

Our <u>Goals</u> in life

<u>Patience</u>—a marathon not a sprint

<u>Discipline</u>—pay ourselves first, spend less than we make

3. I can modify and guide my financial behavior with a well-constructed plan.

4. A plan has Values, Vision, Goals, Strategies, Activities, Milestones.

5. A plan needs PERSONAL ACCOUNTABILITY.

What next?

1. Get around TO IT.

2. With Jen, visit a financial advisor.

# Epilogue

I GUIDED OUR FORD SUV down the mountain, through the snow, toward the hotel. The kids watched a movie on the DVD player in the backseat, and Jennifer read a novel in the front. This was our third trip to Telluride, a local ski area, and Madison and Alex were better skiers than we were. I couldn't believe how those meetings with Aunt Katherine had changed our lives. After the meetings, Jen and I met with a financial advisor and developed an ongoing relationship. From that point on we no longer winged it—we established our values, we actually set and constantly reviewed our goals, and we stayed committed to our plan. Our advisor helped us develop it—we actually clarified our values and set goals, and he guided us to update it frequently. All of that planning had enabled us to take vacations we never would have been able to afford.

Jen turned to the kids in the back. "Are you going to ski tomorrow," she asked, "or snowboard?"

Madison called from the backseat. "Snowboard!" she said excitedly.

"Ski!" Alex answered.

At twelve and fifteen, our girls would wisk down the mountain in the ski suits we had bought them last Christmas and wait for us at the bottom. It would take Jennifer and me another minute to catch up with them; they'd be laughing hysterically. The annual vacation to Telluride was something we'd wanted to do for years, and Jennifer and I had finally saved up enough to do it—the past three years in a row. Now it had become our tradition, complete with the annual snowball fight in the trees on the last run of the day, followed by the sharing of a giant chocolate chip cookie I seemed to always have in my pocket on those occasions. I looked at Jennifer and smiled.

"Can you believe this?" she said, tears welling in her eyes. "Can you believe we are able to live like this, to take our kids on vacation, and spend time together as a family?"

"There was a time I wasn't sure we'd ever be able to live like this," I said.

"Why?" asked Madison from the backseat. "Live like what?"

I cleared my throat. "Well, Maddie, your mom and I had to make some tough decisions when you were in kindergarten to be able to afford to live like this. We had to make financial decisions that would help us create a legacy. We had to stop spending so much money and start saving."

"Do you know what a legacy is?" Jennifer asked.

"No," the girls said in unison.

"A legacy is what you'll leave behind for your own kids and their kids. It's what you'll be known for."

"I don't get it," Madison said.

"It's your plan for your future," Jennifer said. "Your legacy is your reputation, your financial future, your vision, attitude, and actions all rolled into one. I guess the best way to describe your legacy is to envision a treasure chest that you've buried in the snow. When the snow thaws, and someone finds the treasure chest—what is it that will be inside?"

"What's inside your treasure chest," I said, "is whatever you've put there for someone else to find. It might be gold or silver or a love letter. It's your gift to the world and to others."

"Does everyone have a legacy?" Alex asked.

"Yes," I said. "For instance, your Aunt Katherine left a legacy that we'll always remember. She was kindhearted, giving to others. She saved her money so that she could help those less fortunate, and she also saved so she could travel and see the world. Her legacy was also helping us to build our legacy."

"She taught us how to view things so we could save, and plan for our financial future."

"I save my allowance," Madison said.

"And I have five dollars in my room to give to church at the end of the month," said Alex.

Jennifer smiled. "I'm glad we taught you that," she said. "Giving and saving are important. You'll reap rewards from good financial behaviors your entire life."

"So we can keep taking vacations like this one?" Madison asked, grinning.

"Yes," I said. "Your mom and I have a financial advisor who taught us the importance of following a budget, but Aunt Katherine was the one who helped us realize how important that was. Your mom and I make a budget every month, and we follow it. We make sure we have enough money to afford the things you'll need in life."

I pulled the car into the parking lot of the hotel and silenced the engine.

I turned to Jennifer and smiled. The journey had been worth it. There was so much more for us on the road ahead, and now, best of all, we'd be able to afford it. We had planned well. The girls had college funds. Jennifer and

I had planned for retirement, even though it was still years away. Life was good. We had established a sound emergency savings plan, and we had no credit-card debt. Most of all, we had each other.

"Let's have a snowball fight, Dad!" Alex said, bolting from the car, into the snow.

# About the Author

E D BAKER IS A composite of several financial advisors, writers and editors. *The Elephant in the Room: Sharing the Secrets of Real Financial Success* is a compilation of the knowledge and experiences of hundreds of financial advisors who work at First Command Financial Planning and the hundreds of thousands of clients they serve.